Countdown!

ISBN 0-7696-4175-X

Text Copyright © Evans Brothers Ltd. 2005. Illustration Copyright © Evans
Brothers Ltd. 2005. First published by Evans Brothers Limited, 2A Portman
Mansions, Chiltern Street, London W1U 6NR, United Kingdom. This edition
published under license from Zero to Limited. All rights reserved. Printed in
China. This edition published in 2005 by Gingham Dog Press, an imprint of
School Specialty Publishing, a member of the School Specialty Family.

Library of Congress-in-Publication Data is on file with the publisher.

Send all inquiries to:
School Specialty Publishing
8720 Orion Place
Columbus, OH 43240-2111

ISBN 0-7696-4175-X

1 2 3 4 5 6 7 8 9 10 EVN 10 09 08 07 06 05

Countdown!

By Kay Woodward
Illustrated by Ofra Amit

GINGHAM DOG
P R E S S

Columbus, Ohio

It's time to go to bed.

Ready for the countdown.

Ten: a clean astronaut.

Nine: a shiny spacesuit.

11

Eight: moon
shoes.

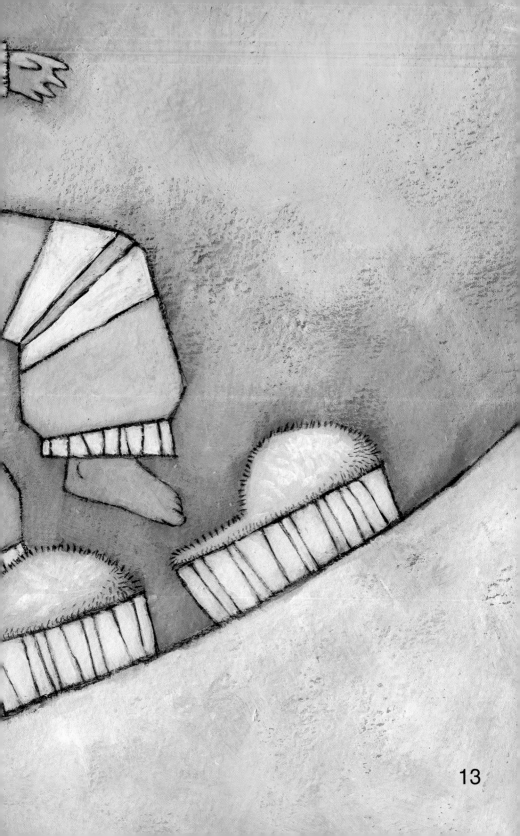

Seven: a rocket book.

Six: space
juice.

Five: my favorite co-pilot.

19

Four: a helmet.

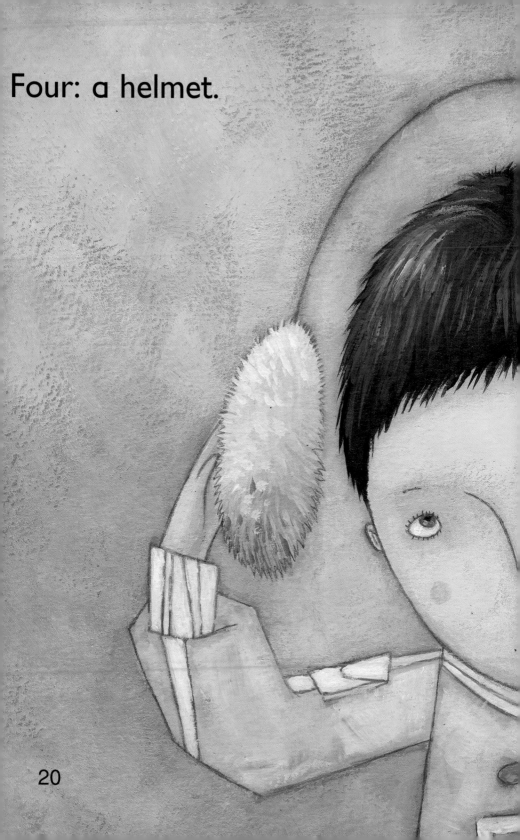

Three: space goggles.

23

Two: a walkie-talkie.

One: My own
spaceship.

Zero.

Zzzzz!

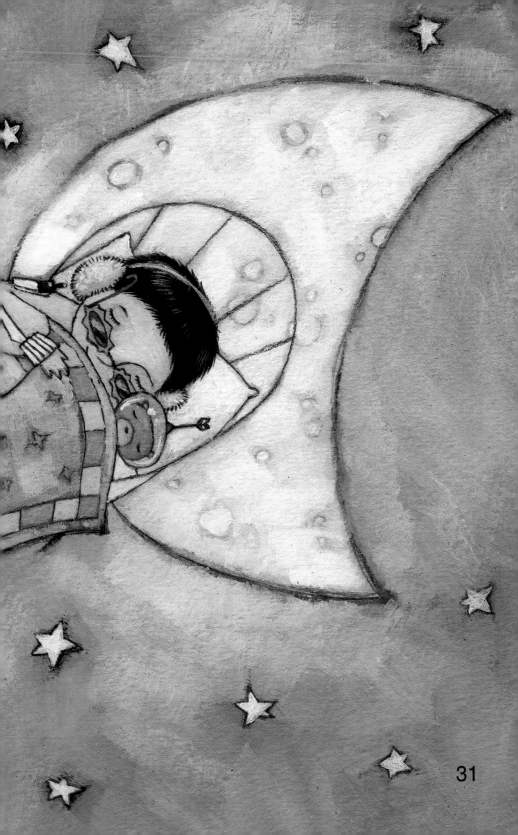

31

Words I Know

time	shoes
ready	rocket
clean	space
moon	juice

Think About It!

1. What is a countdown?

2. How do you know that the little boy likes things about space?

3. What happened after zero?

The Story and You

1. Can you think of a time when you counted down? Why did you count down?

2. Why do people count down for special things?

3. What things do you usually gather when you get ready for bed?